BUCKS ARENA

MARCUS CENTER FOR THE PERFORMING ARTS

URBAN ECOLOGY CENTER

THE MILWAUKEE THEATRE

LAKEFRONT BREWERY

BRONZE FONZ

MILWAUKEE CITY HALL

MILWAUKEE PUBLIC MUSEUM

THE PFISTER HOTEL

MILWAUKEE PUBLIC LIBRARY

HISTORIC THIRD WARD

For Patti and Patrick Doughman,
Pals
—Barb

To Bruce
—Renée

Text Copyright © 2019 Barbara Joosse • Illustration Copyright © 2019 Renée Graef • Design Copyright © 2019 Sleeping Bear Press • All rights reserved. No part of this book may be reproduced in any manner without the express written consent of the publisher, except in the case of brief excerpts in critical reviews and articles. • All inquiries should be addressed to: Sleeping Bear Press™ • 2395 South Huron Parkway, Suite 200, Ann Arbor, MI 48104 www.sleepingbearpress.com © Sleeping Bear Press • Printed and bound in the United States • 10 9 8 7 6 5 4 3 2 1 • Library of Congress Cataloging-in-Publication Data • Names: Joosse, Barbara M., author. • Graef, Renée, illustrator. • Title: Lulu & Rocky in Milwaukee / written by Barbara Joosse ; illustrated by Renée Graef. • Other titles: Lulu and Rocky in Milwaukee • Description: Ann Arbor, MI : Sleeping Bear Press, 2019. • Series: Our city adventures ; Book 1 • Identifiers: LCCN 2018037174 • ISBN 9781534110175 (hardcover) • Subjects: LCSH: Milwaukee (Wis.)—Guidebooks—Juvenile literature. • Children—Travel—Wisconsin—Milwaukee—Guidebooks—Juvenile literature. • Classification: LCC F589.M63 J66 2019 • DDC 917.75/95—dc23 • LC record available at https://lccn.loc.gov/2018037174

THIRD WARD

N
W   E
S

HARLEY-DAVIDSON MUSEUM

A purple envelope arrives.

Dear Lulu,
Are you and Pufferson ready for three days of adventure? Take the Lake Express to Milwaukee. Then head to the Pfister Hotel. Rocky will meet you there.

Aunt Fancy

Lulu Fox

Rocky's my cousin AND best friend.
He gets his invitation by e-mail.

Pufferson and I pack in one second.
Then we board this humongous boat called
a ferry and start crossing Lake Michigan.

Pufferson checks out the map and circles
the bathrooms on the boat, just in case.
Then he plans our itinerary. I follow the
smell of popcorn to the snack bar.

At the Pfister Hotel there's a doorman whose name is Norman. Norman is tall and I'm pretty sure his eyebrows are wooly bear caterpillars.

"Welcome to the Pfister!"

There's Rocky—Mr. Crazypants!
First we bear-hug and fox-box.
Then we LOOK.

There's gold everywhere and everyone smells like perfume. There are angels on the ceiling and I think I'm in heaven.

Rocky holds his breath.
He doesn't like perfume.

Now it's time to explore!
We use canoes from the Urban Ecology
Center and see Milwaukee from the river.

We're starving. Pufferson knows just where to go—
the Historic Third Ward! Fried cheese curds taste
like melted sunshine.

Back at the hotel, Norman says fried
cheese curds are the bee's knees . . .
which means he likes them.

The next day, we take selfies with the Bronze Fonz . . .

climb 84 steps at North Point Lighthouse . . .

and pet a spiny fish-monster called a lake sturgeon at Discovery World.

Then we gear up and burn rubber on our Knucklehead motorcycle at the Harley-Davidson Museum.

We text pictures to Aunt Fancy and she sends us a thumbs-up.

Pufferson says we MUST have a fish fry, so we go to Lakefront Brewery, which is busy and dizzy. Then the polka band plays . . .

and everyone dances in bubbles.

Back at the hotel, we blow bubbles to Norman.
Norman says bubbles are just the ticket . . .
which means he likes them.

Today's our lakefront day!
There are a million things to do.
We pick surrey bikes!

Whew! We drink from a water fountain, which Milwaukee people call a bubbler. Then it's time for inspiration, so we head to the Milwaukee Art Museum.

We are inspired.

On the roof of the museum, there's something called a brise soleil, which looks like huge white wings, folded up. We watch the wings open slowly, like a swan's. Like in *Swan Lake*.

And I feel like I'm riding the swan!
Higher than the clouds!
Higher than the wind!

That night, we paint our day.
Rocky paints a surrey bike and I paint me,
flying on a great white swan. Pufferson paints blobs.

In the morning, it's time to go home.
We give our paintings to Norman so he'll remember us.
Norman says, "How could I forget?"

He winks.
"You're the cat's pajamas". . .
which means he likes us.

We video chat with Aunt Fancy. THANK YOU!!

Then Rocky and I fox-box goodbye. From the boat, Pufferson and I wave to Norman, the fish monster, the surrey bikes, and the great white swan. We wave goodbye to Milwaukee . . .

and Milwaukee waves back.

MILWAUKEE

MORE TO KNOW!

Milwaukee is known for super-friendly people and beautiful parks with lots to do. Nicknames for the city include Cream City (because of some buildings' cream-colored bricks), City of Festivals (because of the many festivals held every year), and Brew City (because of its long history of brewing beer).

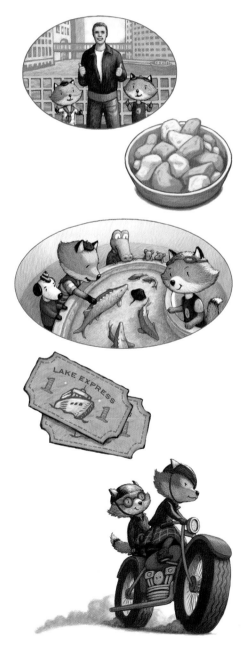

The **Bronze Fonz**, a pop art statue on the Milwaukee RiverWalk, is a favorite selfie spot. The Fonz is a replica of the character Arthur Fonzarelli from the television show *Happy Days*.

A **bubbler** is the word Milwaukeeans use for a water fountain.

Cheese curds are very, very fresh cheese pieces—and they squeak when you chew them! Warm, fried cheese curds melt in your mouth.

Discovery World Science and Technology Museum is a hands-on family museum that explores technology and freshwater science, including a freshwater tank where you can pet a lake sturgeon. You can also board the tall ship *Denis Sullivan*, look inside a mummy (using a CT scan), and more.

The **Harley-Davidson Museum** has lots of motorcycle activities for kids. You can put on Harley gear and rev the motor on a Knuckle-head motorcycle or build your own bike in the virtual chopper shop.

The **Lake Express**, a high-speed auto ferry, crosses Lake Michigan in two and a half hours. It takes four big engines to carry passengers, cars, motorcycles, and trailers 118 miles from Muskegon, Michigan, to Milwaukee, Wisconsin.

Lake sturgeon can live from 55–150 years, and can grow to over 7 feet long and weigh close to 300 pounds!

Lake Michigan is cold and HUGE—22,300 square miles! The lake acts as an air conditioner to keep Milwaukee cool all summer long.

Lakefront Brewery, a microbrewery on the Milwaukee River, has one of the best Friday night fish fries in town! After dinner, you can dance as a band plays polkas.

The **Milwaukee Art Museum** on Lake Michigan is inspiring inside and out. The breathtaking Burke Brise Soleil is a huge winglike structure (its wingspan is similar to that of a Boeing 747) that opens in the morning and closes at night. It has a sensor that automatically closes the wings if winds reach 23 miles per hour.

The **Milwaukee RiverWalk**, a unique urban outdoor gallery, is 20 blocks long and includes more than 20 sculptures along the Milwaukee River. There are lots of outdoor patios along the way.

North Point Lighthouse was important to maritime Milwaukee as it guided ships on Lake Michigan. Keepers and their families lived at the lighthouse to make sure the light was always working. The top offers an amazing 360-degree view of Milwaukee and the lake.

The **Pfister Hotel** opened its doors in 1893, so it is more than 125 years old. It is one of the most elegant hotels in Milwaukee . . . and also one of the friendliest!

The **Historic Third Ward**, one of Milwaukee's most creative hubs, is home to trendy boutiques, restaurants, galleries, and the indoor Milwaukee Public Market.

The **Urban Ecology Center** connects people with nature in the city from three separate locations. Find out about the birds, frogs, bats, turtles, snakes, and mammals that share the city with you.

Veterans Park, along Milwaukee's lakefront, offers lots of things to do, including kite flying, surrey bikes, turbo bikes, handcycles, Segways, paddleboats, and kayaks.

Next time we visit we want to: sail on the *Denis Sullivan*, cheer for the Brew City Bruisers roller derby, see a play at First Stage Children's Theater, walk through a tropical jungle at The Domes, explore Science City at the Betty Brinn Children's Museum, and see the buffalo stampede at the Milwaukee Public Museum. Also, we want to eat frozen custard at Leon's.